POLICE ★ PUP
Hershey

Ready to
Lend a Paw

THERAPY
DOG

Based on a True Tail
Constable Val Hoglund
Illustrated by Constable Liv Vors

Edited by Jaimie Hoglund and Bryony van der Merwe
Narrated by Hershey

Dedication

This book is dedicated to the youth who taught Copper how to be a better police officer, and to Inspector Dan, who believes in those youth and Hershey's ability to help them.

This book is proudly supported by the Edmonton Police Association and the Edmonton Community Foundation.

First published in 2022

Written by Constable Val Hoglund
Illustrated by Constable Liv Vors
Edited by Jaimie Hoglund and Bryony van der Merwe

ISBN: 978-1-7781199-0-3
Available on Amazon.ca

Contents

Foreword

Dogs are wonderful animals as they can be kind, take care of us, snuggle, and make us laugh, even if we don't have a dog ourselves. Some dogs have special roles and are good at helping people.

In this book, you will meet Hershey, a police therapy dog. He helps children, especially when they might be having some problems. You will discover how much Hershey loves his job.

This story is not only about Hershey, but also Constable Val, or as Hershey calls her, Copper! Constable Val is the police officer who trained Hershey. I know this because I have met Constable Val and Hershey many times, and I love how children feel safe and important when they meet with them. Constable Val and Hershey assist children if they are scared, sad, confused, or worried. Children then may be able to understand all the different feelings they can have inside when they have been hurt or when life is hard. Sometimes these children find it difficult to talk about their feelings, and that is where Hershey comes in, because starting with a therapy dog feels less scary.

Constable Val and Hershey are an amazing team.

In this book, you will learn how police officers don't only enforce the law, but are beneficial in many ways, including making time to talk to children. When you get to know them, they're not scary – even when they're wearing a police uniform! You will also discover how smart and dedicated Hershey is, and read about how he was able to give support to Robyn and many other children.

After reading this book, I hope you will find it easier to talk to police officers and maybe a therapy dog, if you ever need to. I believe you will enjoy this book and learn lots from Hershey and Copper...oops, I mean Constable Val!

Peter Smyth
Social Worker

★
CHAPTER 1
Copper's Problem

"**H**ershey, come!" my human sister called out to me.

I was a three-month-old border collie puppy. Snuggling with my human sister while she read to me was one of my favourite activities.

Border collies are herding dogs. Mostly, they're black and white, and hyperactive, but not me. I'm brown and white, and very calm. What can I say? I'm unique!

My human sister loved how I lay still beside her for hours while she read her favourite books to me. "Hershey, you'd make a very good therapy dog. I've heard of therapy dogs helping people in places like schools and hospitals. Maybe you could help Mom at her work."

My human mom is a police officer. Her name is Constable Val, but I call her Copper. I have great respect for the work my police mom does, but I also like to joke around with her because she is my mom.

Copper has been a policewoman for many, many years: thirty, in fact. I like to tease her about how old she is, but she still looks young and has the energy of a kid. I guess that's why she likes working with kids so much. Copper works with children in a Kindergarten to Grade 9 school. Having a police officer in a school builds strong relationships between young people and the police.

When I was about seven months old, Copper came home from work in her police uniform for the first time. I didn't recognize her. She looked like a scary stranger. I lowered my ears and slowly backed away, keeping my gaze fixed on her, and then I barked! I was confused and asked myself, "Who's that? Where's Copper?"

The scary stranger smiled and sat down on the floor beside me, and Copper's voice said, "It's really me, Hershey."

I kept my head low, and my tail tucked between my legs to let my police mom know what I thought of this *uniform*. I sniffed her up and down and then, very cautiously, curled up beside her.

"Many of the children in my school are also afraid of police uniforms, Hershey," Copper said, sounding frustrated and sad.

After a lot of petting and cuddles, Copper stood up and found Beaver, one of my favourite stuffies.

"Let's play fetch!"

She knew I loved that game.

While Copper and I played, she explained that police officers wear a uniform so people can see who they are. This makes it easier for them to help people.

I was nervous about all the tools on her belt. But Copper told me that she only used them as a last resort when trying to resolve conflict.

"The best tool I have is verbal communication, or talking," Copper said. That made me feel much better.

"I understand why the kids are afraid of your police uniform. I am too," I admitted.

Copper frowned and crossed her arms in frustration. "I want the kids to know that police officers do more than just enforce the law. I wish I had a tool that shows how I help people."

I lay down on my dog bed that night, thinking about Copper's problem. I recalled what my human sister had said to me when I was a young pup. I wondered if a herding dog like me could become a therapy dog.

That night, my paws twitched while I dreamed of helping Copper at her work.

★
CHAPTER 2
My Dream

A few months later, when I was about nine months old, Copper was cooking up one of her famous rancher breakfasts for my human sister and brother. I gazed up at Copper with my sweet puppy dog eyes. She looked around to make sure nobody was watching and then slipped me a few pieces of bacon.

While Copper was at work every day, I was also very busy. We lived on a sheep farm just outside the city, and one day it would be my responsibility to protect our flock. In the meantime, I needed to learn everything about herding sheep.

I was born at the farm next door, where my dog family lived. Hershey Senior, my dog father, was the best herding dog in our community. Every day, I trotted over to him for my herding lesson. In the beginning, I enjoyed the lessons, but soon I started to feel that I was destined to do something different in life.

Hershey Senior had done his best to spark a passion in me for herding. He knew, however, that I didn't look or act like a herding dog. My fur coat has a lot of white which made me blend in too well with the sheep. They didn't notice that I was even there to protect them. I also didn't have the drive to chase after a herd of sheep. Most of all, herding was boring and unfulfilling.

I wanted to help children! I decided to follow my human sister's advice about becoming a therapy dog. I could escape the herding life that didn't want me – and vice versa. I could be the tool that Copper needed!

After our delicious breakfast, I asked Copper, "What if I were to become a therapy dog? Could I be a good tool for you to *help* people?"

"A police therapy dog?" Copper's eyes widened, and she stopped washing dishes.

"Ruff!" I barked loudly in agreement.

"That's a great idea! Hershey Senior has told us that you aren't very interested in herding, and we've been unsure of what to do. This would solve both problems!"

I couldn't believe what I was hearing! I danced around Copper's legs in excitement.

"Great!" Copper clasped her hands together and laughed with a sparkle in her eyes. "The kids could really benefit if I have a loveable and furry partner. Plus, you're very obedient because of Hershey Senior's lessons."

I instantly sat down, still as a statue.

"Your dog brother, Aero, on Hershey Senior's farm, can take over your sheep herding responsibilities for now. He has the energy of ten dogs," Copper laughed.

My heart pumped loudly with joy at the possibility of helping my police mom at her work. I knew how much Copper loved being a police officer. I also knew how frustrating it was that her uniform frightened some kids and prevented them from getting the help they needed.

The next day, Copper drove me to her police station to meet the police family she was so proud of. But as soon as I saw the police officers in the parking lot, the fur on my back rose. I started feeling anxious, like I had when Copper first came home in her uniform.

I pressed my nose up against our car window and had a terrifying feeling in my tummy. "Look at all of those police officers in their scary uniforms!"

Just then, two officers walked closely by our car. I picked up my blanket with my teeth and threw it over my body, hiding underneath it.

Shivering from fear, I whimpered, "My dream of becoming a police therapy dog is turning into a nightmare."

★
CHAPTER 3
That Scary Uniform

Copper gently opened the back door of our vehicle and slowly sat down beside me. My security blanket offered me protection from my greatest fear: that scary uniform. My police mom put her hand under my quivering blanket and tenderly petted my fur.

Copper told me a story of how she overcame *her* biggest fear: police training. She said her training sergeant was super scary.

"Hershey, my goal was to become a police officer, and I wasn't going to let anything get in my way."

Copper suggested that when we walked into the police station, I should show the police officers that I was afraid.

"If they know you're scared, they'll be gentle and understand that they have to earn your trust." She continued to pet me. "This is my police family, Hershey. All families need a dog. Follow your dreams! Let's go in."

I nudged my head out from under my blanket. Copper's warm smile inspired me to take one more look at the 'cop shop', as she liked to call it. My police mom's story encouraged me to do my very best. I truly wanted to be a therapy dog for Copper. It was my *dream*.

I climbed out of my blanket and looked at the cop shop. I hoped that the officers were nice, regular people underneath those scary clothes. I took a deep breath and then sighed my anxiety out.

Copper's smile grew bigger. "Are you ready to go in, Hersh?"

I nodded.

She kissed me on the top of my head. She always does that to show me how much she loves me. I licked her cheek to say it back.

We slowly eased into the police station through the front doors. I flattened my ears to let everyone know that I was concerned. I stayed close to my police mom and tucked my tail tightly between my legs.

I'm generally timid around men, and I had never seen so many men before, especially so many in police uniforms.

When we arrived at Copper's office, her squad shrieked with surprise, "Look at the cute puppy!"

Copper's squad was composed of both men and women. One of the ladies smelled like a sweet garden, which was very comforting. I am more of a ladies' dog. To my delight, the whole squad was thrilled to meet me.

One of Copper's high-ranking bosses, Inspector Dan, also came over to see me. "Is this the hound you want to train to be a therapy dog, Constable Val?" he firmly inquired in a growly voice.

"Yes, Sir! I believe that 'human's best friend' can help me earn the trust of more kids in my school." Copper smiled at me while she petted my head.

"I hope you've done your research, Constable Val." Inspector Dan looked at his watch as if we were holding him back from something important. Then he pointed a pen at Copper. "I'm not entirely sold on this idea, but I'll approve of you and your herding dog to begin training together."

I sat very still but couldn't stop my tail from wagging eagerly.

Inspector Dan looked down at me. "Your manners are impressive for a young pup." Then he pointed his pen at me, and my tail stopped wagging. "I'll give you *one* chance. Don't blow it."

I offered Inspector Dan a paw to shake, but instead, **he turned back toward Copper.**

"Put your furball through obedience training and then animal therapy school. When you're done, bring him to work for one week for him to prove his value."

"Yes, Sir. Thank you, Sir!" Copper was blushing. I could tell she was trying to hold back her enthusiasm.

"If your farm dog successfully completes both training programs and actually ends up helping some kids during that workweek, I might decide to offer him a job." Inspector Dan walked down the hall rapidly while murmuring, "This better not be a waste of time and money."

Copper and I were thrilled!

Outside in the parking lot, Copper shot both hands high in the air and made some cool moves, like a football player who just scored a touchdown. I stood up on my hind legs, doing a little dance of my own.

"Yessss!" Copper screeched and gave me a high five. "I knew you could do it, Hershey!"

I thanked my police mom for encouraging me to face my fear. I rewarded her by licking her chin a lot.

We both believed I would make a difference for the kids Copper worked with. She knew that deep down, Inspector Dan also believed it.

Copper wasted no time. She immediately signed me up for obedience training. It was once a week for two months. It came naturally to me and was far more rewarding than herding lessons. I worked hard and paid attention, knowing that I only had this one chance.

I was almost a year old by then and practically full grown. On the last day of obedience training, I was awarded a certificate.

"You aced it, Hershey!" said Copper, inspired. "Animal therapy school, here we come!"

I showed my certificate to my dog family and told them the next step was animal therapy school.

I even told my stuffies, Moose, Beaver and Bear, that I was going to school!

★
CHAPTER 4
Animal Therapy School

On my first day at school, I was so excited that I accidentally peed on the floor. I also kept forgetting to raise my paw when I wanted to speak. Copper had told me that the teaching part of school would only last three days. She warned me to pay close attention because it would race by faster than a Jack Russell terrier.

Our instructor's name was Mrs. Katz. At first, I thought cats were her favourite animals, but she told us that she loved all animals, not just cats, as her name is pronounced.

Mrs. Katz was a short, round, older lady with grey hair. She wore black-rimmed glasses on the tip of her nose in the shape of a cat's eyes.

There were many different dogs in our class, and to my surprise, there was also a pot-bellied pig! In our first lesson, Mrs. Katz asked us to introduce ourselves and encouraged us to share any tricks that we knew. She suggested that a good sense of humour may be helpful for some clients we would be working with.

"My name is Smooch," the little pig announced. Then he performed a remarkable trick – he backed his rear hooves up against the wall, so he was only standing on his front legs. He also played a toy piano and took a bow afterward. I had no idea pigs were so bright. Smooch inspired me to learn some clever tricks for the kids in Copper's school. *What a fun way to begin school,* I thought to myself.

Later that day, we watched videos of therapy dogs in hospitals, and Mrs. Katz taught us how to gently approach humans whether they are standing, lying down, or sitting.

Copper and I had to write an essay explaining why I wanted to be a therapy dog from my point of view. I told my police mom to include: *I want to help kids. I love how happy they get when they see me and pet me.* I also told Copper to say that I have a great work ethic. I signed the essay with a big Hershey paw print when she finished.

"Paws crossed that we get a great mark!" I smiled up at Copper.

On our second day, Mrs. Katz put us through numerous tests. One of the tests was to see our reactions towards an eager person who petted us too roughly. The eager person walked up to me while I was sitting quietly beside Copper's leg. She bent down and rubbed my ears really hard while yelling how happy she was to see me. I sat there patiently and kept still.

I looked up at Copper, and she winked at me. "Good job, Hershey."

Copper told me that I was one *hot* dog. I translated this to mean that I did very well on all my tests that day, instead of being someone's lunch food.

On our last teaching day, Mrs. Katz told us that most of our learning would come from working in the field. At first, I thought of my herding field, but then Copper said the teacher meant our chosen field of *work – police work*.

Mrs. Katz pushed up her glasses that were low on her nose. "I've assigned each of you two field trips. By the time you return later today, I'll have your grades ready. How well you do on your field trips, combined with your grades, will determine if you graduate from animal therapy school."

I thought to myself, "Field trips sound so exciting! I love school!" I was really interested to see the different places where therapy dogs work.

Before we left for our first field trip, Copper surprised me with a therapy dog training vest. Initially, I was afraid of it and thought it might hurt me!

My vest was blue with white writing on it. "Therapy dog in training," Copper read aloud.

The fur all over my body stuck straight out.

"Come, Hershey, try it on." Copper waved at me to come closer, but I wasn't so sure. I thought I was perfect the way I was. But Copper was patient, and eventually, I did as she asked. She took a photograph and showed it to me. I did look very professional in my new vest. I decided that if my police mom could wear a uniform, I could easily wear a vest.

I was ready to go! I was going to do everything in my power to impress Mrs. Katz so I could graduate from her animal therapy school.

★
CHAPTER 5
A Tricky Treat

Our first field trip was to a building filled with police detectives and social workers. A facility dog worked there. Her name was Marley, and she was a beautiful golden Labrador. I felt warm and happy next to her.

Marley and her handler, Annie, met us at the reception desk and gave us a tour of their facility. I was relieved that the police detectives wore business suits instead of uniforms. The office smelled like coffee, juice and candy.

There were stuffed toys, or 'stuffies' as I like to call them, such as teddy bears and zebras, in every office. Seeing those brand-new toys made me think I should have brought some of my well-loved stuffies from home. Those toys probably didn't even smell like a dog.

While Copper spoke with Annie in the hallway, I followed Marley to her office, where she showed me to her water bowl and cookie dish. We sat on her soft dog bed while she told me about her important job.

I gazed into Marley's beautiful brown eyes while she spoke softly. "I help children feel comfortable about meeting a police detective. It can be difficult for children to talk about something they saw or something that happened to them."

I was impressed and sat very straight while I listened to Marley. I said, "I feel good just sitting beside you and listening to you. I can imagine how good you are at helping children."

Marley nodded at me. "Thank you, Hershey. I'm like a Compassion Bodyguard or a Guardian Angel."

I almost told Marley she was as pretty as an angel but decided against it. I wanted to remain professional. Instead, I said, "You're very inspiring, Marley." I held back an urge to pick up her paw and kiss it.

I thanked Marley for sharing her dog treats and water. While leaving Marley's office, I knew I wanted to be just like her.

I met up with Copper in the hallway, where she was saying goodbye to Annie. Copper walked over to the elevator and pushed the down button. I expressed to her how happy I was to have met Marley.

"I can't wait to do good work like Marley. I was born to be a Compassion Bodyguard!" I rubbed myself back and forth against Copper's legs with anticipation of graduating from animal therapy school.

"I'm glad that Marley had such a positive influence on you. I learned a lot from Annie, too." Copper quietly clapped her hands together. Copper was vibrating with excitement and grinning from ear to ear. "There's a great need for therapy dogs in many areas of police work."

I woofed twice in agreement.

"Our next field trip is to a senior's centre, Hershey. Mrs. Katz wants to see how you do in a busy building with a lot of people living in it." Copper sounded like she was on a fun adventure and couldn't wait to get to the next part.

We picked up my human sister on the way. She was excited to see my training in action.

When we arrived, I saw a lot of seniors playing crib and shuffleboard. I smelled scotch mints in most rooms we went into, and sometimes I even smelled scotch. A few seniors gave me treats while Copper wasn't looking. They pressed one finger to their lips, making the 'shh' sign while looking sideways at my police mom. What a fun place to visit, I thought.

My human sister sat down, and I jumped on her lap. While Copper spoke to a staff member, we visited with one of the seniors.

The senior said, "You are the calmest border collie I've ever seen." He stroked my fur gently with a smile on his face.

He loved how I curled up quietly on my sister's lap. The friendly senior reached into his pocket and gave me a treat. I licked it up. Yuck, it tasted terrible! I immediately felt heavy and woozy.

When Copper returned and saw how groggy I was, she cried out, "What's wrong?"

A supervisor at the senior's home had seen what happened. She walked over to us.

"Doug gave your dog a pill," she explained to Copper. Then she told my police mom to always stay by my side when we were working together.

"Seniors often have medication on them and can innocently want to share pills," she continued. "Luckily, the medicine that Doug gave to Hershey isn't harmful. Hershey may want to have a short nap."

While Copper carried me out to our car, I hoped this tricky treat wouldn't prevent me from graduating from animal therapy school.

I tried my hardest to stay awake, but soon I was dreaming of being just like Marley.

★
CHAPTER 6
Last Chance

When Copper put her car in park at Mrs. Katz's Animal Therapy School, I woke up feeling refreshed. It was the end of the week, and Copper and I were about to find out if I had graduated from school.

We walked up the sidewalk toward the front door where, surprisingly, Inspector Dan was waiting for us. I detected anger, so I tucked my tail between my legs as Copper and I approached.

Before we arrived, Mrs. Katz had already received feedback about our field trips and had told Inspector Dan about the medication I had swallowed.

"How could you be so reckless, Constable Val?" he yelled. He looked really mad. Then he glared down at me and said, "You had *one* chance, and you blew it!"

I lowered my ears.

Inspector Dan fixed his gaze back on Copper and admitted, "I've invested a lot of money in this mutt's training and was actually considering hiring him."

Copper's boss then spoke so fast I couldn't keep up. When his face went red, I squeezed my eyes shut. I heard something about "...animal endangerment..." and "...possible suspension of your job..." and then finally, Inspector Dan raised his voice even more and spat out "...one LAST chance! KEEP AN EYE ON YOUR DOG!"

I opened one eye, and before Inspector Dan stormed away, he thrust a piece of paper at Copper. She scrambled to grasp it before it fell to the ground. Inspector Dan's police car lowered significantly as his heavy body slumped into the driver's seat. He slammed the door shut before Copper could squeak out the words, "Yes...Sir! THANK YOU...Sir!"

I was afraid to make eye contact with Copper. Eventually, I looked up, and to my surprise, she was smiling. I lifted my ears and waited for her to tell me why she wasn't shaking in her police boots.

"Don't worry, Hershey, his bark is worse than his bite," as she waved at nothing in the air. She often does the wave thing. "It was an honest mistake, and we learned from it, right?"

I agreed. And at least we had been given a second chance, and I hadn't been sent home.

"If he didn't believe in us, he would have sent you home," she said casually.

I wagged my tail in agreement. I loved it when we read each other's minds.

I was still a bit shaken, and I thought I was in the doghouse for sure, but Copper made it all better. I gave her hand a Hershey kiss to thank her for being such an awesome mom.

Copper squinted at the piece of paper that Inspector Dan had shoved at her. She screamed, "Hersh! You graduated from school!"

She held up the certificate from Mrs. Katz's Animal Therapy School for me to see. "Hershey, Certified Therapy Dog," she read out loud, beaming with pride.

I howled like it was full moon. Copper gave me a big hug, and we both looked closer at my certificate. Mrs. Katz's signature was beside a picture of Copper and me.

We went inside the animal therapy school and celebrated everyone's graduation. I was thrilled that Smooch had graduated as well.

I couldn't wait to share the good news with my dog family. News spreads fast in the dog community, and I wanted to be the one to tell them.

Once home, I sprinted straight over to my dog family's farm. Everyone, except Hershey Senior, smothered me in kisses. "You're the first pup in the family to have an education!" they all woofed.

Hershey Senior had remained lying down on his dog bed. He showed no emotion as he slowly rose. He walked over and stood in front of me. The rest of my dog family grew silent.

"It's a fine thing to have an education; that's why I taught you the exemplary obedience you are proud of today. It's another thing to do the work and save lives. I hope you're up for the task, son."

As my wise dog father turned away from me, he told me I'd always have a job on his farm if I needed one. I promised myself that I would be successful with my education and make a difference in as many kids' lives as possible.

I hoped I could keep that promise.

★
CHAPTER 7
One Set of Clothes

It was Sunday, and I had just woken up from a doggie nap at home. I found myself napping a lot to recover from the exciting days of animal therapy school. Napping had been forbidden in school, and they even put up 'No Napping' signs to remind us.

I was staring at my graduation certificate above my bed when Copper told me that I was the youngest pup ever to have graduated from Mrs. Katz's Animal Therapy School.

"Normally, animals don't graduate until they are TWO years old, Hershey," Copper said proudly. "You're only one year old."

Copper then reminded me of something that made my heart beat really fast.

"Remember when Inspector Dan said that if you graduate from your training, he will give you one week to prove yourself at my work?

"Yesssssssss," I said nervously. Those scary uniforms came rushing back to my mind.

"Tomorrow, you get to come to work with me!" Copper squeaked like a mouse and held her closed fists tightly under her chin. She was smiling like she did on the day she adopted me.

Copper then noticed my ears droop. She recognized my fearful look and leaned over to console me.

"Don't worry, Hershey. We'll balance our time between the police station and my school," Copper said encouragingly. "You won't always be around cops."

I cringed at the thought of those scary uniforms. However, my heart was full with the idea of going with Copper to her work. After months of preparation, I would finally get to help kids!

"We only have one week to impress Inspector Dan."

I hung on to every word Copper was saying.

"Now that we're working together, your day will start early. When my alarm clock goes off in the morning, you won't have the luxury of sleeping in."

I'd have to start my usual up-dog and down-dog yoga stretches (that Hershey Senior had taught me) much earlier than I was used to.

Then Copper looked at me from head to tail. "You only have one set of clothes, Hershey," referring to my fur coat, "so I'll groom you every day before work."

Looking good is important but smelling good is too. After breakfast, my teeth would need to be brushed. My human brother offered to do that for me.

"Kids won't want to get close to you if you have stinky doggie breath, Hershey." I assumed he spoke from experience, but I didn't question him. I wish I could have taken a great big bone to Copper's work to chew on instead.

Then Copper instructed, "Every child you meet will be different. I'll introduce you, and you take it from there."

I lifted my ears and tilted my head to the side, listening with great interest.

"Listen carefully to their situation, and your trusty instincts will guide you to do the right thing for them." Copper sounded like she knew exactly what she was talking about.

I'm an expert at paying close attention to humans. I couldn't wait to start helping kids.

I went to bed Sunday night thinking about my big first day. I'd be riding in the front seat of a police car!

★
CHAPTER 8
Herding is Lame

Monday was the first day of my workweek with Copper. I was eager and nervous at the same time. I was thrilled to start work, but was still shaking in my fur coat.

On our drive in, I turned up the music on the radio. Copper and I sang and howled because we would be helping kids together.

When we parked at the cop shop, I hesitantly jumped out of our car and Copper put on my training vest.

"You'll be so *pawpular*," Copper giggled as she played with my paws. "Everyone is overjoyed it is your first day," Copper promised, "including those scary police officers." She winked at me.

Copper greeted the front desk staff and then held her ID card to a scanner. Copper told me that police stations could have a cold feeling to them, but this was quickly filled with the warm smiles of police officers who care deeply about helping people. The scanner beeped, a green light flashed, and the door to the hallway unlocked. We walked past an exercise room, where some police officers ran on treadmills. Then we passed by an interview room and a lunchroom.

Copper then opened the door to the fingerprinting room, where she introduced me to an officer who worked in the Forensic Identification Section.

"Hello, Hershey," the friendly officer said. "My name is Constable Pete. All employees, even temporary ones, must have their fingerprints and photograph taken. Then, you get your own employee card to scan when you enter the building."

"Fingerprints?" I asked, holding up one of my paws to Constable Pete.

Constable Pete shrugged and laughed. "I guess I'll be taking your pawprints. There's a first for everything, eh, Hershey?"

Constable Pete gently placed each of my front paws on a pad of black ink and then rolled them onto a piece of paper. I recognized my prints from the time I walked across Copper's clean floor with dirty paws.

Once paw-printing was complete, Copper carried me over to a sink where Constable Pete washed the ink off with some orange-scented soap. He then took a picture of my furry face and printed an ID card with my photograph. I felt so important!

We thanked Constable Pete as we left. Copper slid my ID card into the slot on the top of my vest. She looked at me with a cheery expression, rubbing her hands quickly together. "Time to meet Sergeant Smith! He's my direct supervisor."

As we neared Sergeant Smith's office, he looked up, smiled, and waved at us to come in. I thought he looked very fit. He bent down on one knee, holding out his big, strong hand for me to shake.

"Welcome aboard, Police Pup!"

Wow, I loved the sound of that!

"I'm Sergeant Smith. It's so *doggone* nice to meet you," Sergeant Smith chuckled at his own riddle.

I sensed that Sergeant Smith was friendlier than Inspector Dan, but I still hesitantly raised my paw and slowly shook his giant hand. Sergeant Smith had suspected that I might be unsure on my first day, so he had brought a ball from home. He wrote my name on it, and we played fetch in the hallway until I felt comfortable around him.

After the fun game with my police mom's cool sergeant, he kneeled in front of me again. He patted my head while he spoke. "We've never had a therapy dog in our unit before, but we're looking forward to seeing how you can help our kids."

"Me too!" My tail swept back and forth across the floor uncontrollably.

"Having a police officer in a school helps build trusting relationships between young people and the police, but it takes time," Sergeant Smith said in a kind-hearted and fatherly tone of voice. "Constable Val believes that you can speed up that process so kids can get help sooner."

This was exactly what I'd hoped!

He continued, "I think she's right. I'm happy you're here. Now, go settle in, and I'll come to see you in a little while." Sergeant Smith walked back to his desk, singing a song.

Copper and I thanked him, and this time we walked down the hall towards her office. I recognized many of the staff members from my first visit. Laury, a crime reporter clerk, bought me a water dish in the shape of a dog bone. Julianne, the youth worker, gave me a toy with delicious peanut butter inside it. Both of these ladies did not wear a police uniform and were called civilians. I had not realized how many kinds of people were required to run a police station.

Next, I met Copper's squad. There were six of them who sat in the same room with their desks all together. Copper called it a bullpen, but I didn't see any bulls. It seemed like they had a lot of fun together.

One of Copper's squadmates said, "Hey buddy, take your coat off and stay for a while."

Silly human, I thought, I can't take my coat off.

Another one of Copper's squadmates handed around a box of dog cookies so that everyone could take a few treats to keep in their bottom desk drawer for me. I learned to paw at these drawers whenever I wanted a yummy snack.

A little while later, Sergeant Smith cheerfully walked into our bullpen, just as he had promised, whistling a tune. He smiled while he held out his hand for me to sniff and then gave my head a scratch.

"It's time for you to help some children, Police Pup. I think it will make their day to meet you." Sergeant Smith sang some more as he walked back to his office. I think he was happy I was there. I was relieved by how supportive he was.

Then Inspector Dan came by. He didn't even look at me, but I overheard him talking to Copper.

"Are you sure he's ready, Constable Val?" Inspector Dan rigidly inquired. "I need a daily report on his progress, and I expect good results. If he isn't successful in one week, he can go back to herding sheep."

"NOOOOOOOOOOOOO!" I wailed to myself under Copper's desk. Herding is LAME!

I was grateful to be at work with Copper, but all I could think about was our sheep making fun of me if I failed at my dream job.

★
CHAPTER 9
Copper's School

As we were about to leave the police station, I wondered how different it would be to work with children compared to lambs. I'd heard humans say that taking care of children was sometimes like herding sheep. Knowing how hard herding sheep could be, I really hoped that I wouldn't fail at helping kids. I also hoped the children would have many questions about my police mom's handsome and furry new partner.

Copper and I left the cop shop through the rear door and headed to the 'police only' parking area. It was filled with cop cars, vans, trucks and even cop bicycles.

"Which one's yours?" I asked, trying to act cool, but honestly, I could barely contain my happy dance.

"That one!" Copper said playfully. She pressed her key fob, and I heard a honk.

In the very back row, the lights flashed on a Hummer!

"I booked it for your special day, Hershey. You'll never forget your first day of work in this cool whip," Copper said with a kiddish grin. "Jump in!"

"What a sweet ride!" I yelped.

I knew I'd never be in a cooler cop car. As we drove, I stuck my head out the window, drooling all over the side of the Hummer.

When we arrived at Copper's school, the principal greeted me with a box of dog cookies as a welcome gift. I loved working; there were cookies everywhere! Copper giggled and said the cookies were my paycheque.

"We're thrilled you're here, Hershey," said the principal with a sincere smile.

The principal was a tall woman with red, curly hair. She looked about eight dog years old. She kept smiling at me, but my reliable doggie senses told me she didn't want to pet me. I gave her the space she needed. She looked pleased to have me in her school, even if she wasn't a dog lover.

"Come, let me show you around."

We toured the elementary portion of the school. It was an older building and was quite different from the police station. I was overwhelmed by all the different scents. It was also much louder, with hundreds of kids rushing around. Sometimes it was hard to tell where a sound was coming from, so I constantly moved my ears in every direction. A warning bell blared from the ceiling, making me jump, followed by a loud yet muffled voice.

"These announcements happen every hour, Hershey," the soothing principal said when she saw my frightened reaction.

Copper petted my head often during the tour, always sending me a reassuring smile. She knew I was tense. She said it was normal for anyone to be on edge until their surroundings became familiar.

We met giddy students who squealed with delight when they saw me. Copper introduced me to the classrooms, where I received pets from the happy students. My paws were sweaty, but I don't think anybody noticed. The children asked many questions about me, just as I'd hoped.

The principal ended the tour in Copper's office, where Copper took over and thanked the principal. Copper had bought me a new dog bed and water dish. She also had a box of dog cookies on the table and some in her desk bottom drawer. Our office was next to the cafeteria, which smelled very appealing.

I reached into the animal therapy bag that Mrs. Katz suggested Copper carry around with her. I pulled out two of my favourite stuffies, Moose and Beaver, for children to play with when they visited.

After a quick snack and some water, Copper and I walked casually in the hallways. I could tell that lunchtime was approaching because the smell of delicious food wafted from the cafeteria. Copper and I joined some students in the cafeteria, where I found yummy lunch meat that had *accidentally* fallen on the floor.

We joined many classes after lunch, continuing my introduction to the younger students. After the last school bell rang, many of the students I had met patted my head goodbye when they walked out of the school.

A few of them cheerfully yelled,
"See you tomorrow, Hershey!"

It had been great meeting the younger kids. Despite my initial worries, I thought I'd done well. I looked forward to meeting the older kids the next day.

Back in Copper's office, I lay down on my dog bed.

"Great first day today, Hershey. You will get to know the students better as the week goes on." Copper roughed up my fur before sitting at her desk to type up our first progress report for Inspector Dan.

My dream job was happening fur real!

★
CHAPTER 10
Just a Herding Dog

On Tuesday, I was still a little nervous. As Copper and I prepared to go to her work, the fur on the back of my neck stood up again. It does that all by itself, and instantly Copper noticed.

"You can relax, Hershey. We'll be starting today at the school instead of the cop shop."

I was relieved to hear that. It meant Inspector Dan wouldn't be towering over me, and I could focus on the students.

Once at school, we toured the junior high portion so I could meet the older students. They were happy to meet me and liked how I offered them high-fives.

After our tour, we went to Copper's office. When she was there, she liked to leave her door open to welcome any students and staff. While she made a few phone calls, I padded over to the cafeteria to introduce myself to the chef. I was pleasantly surprised when she offered me a sausage. I thanked her, and she told me to come back each day for some delicious food. I trotted back to Copper's office, licking my chops.

As I walked in, Copper smiled, "Hershey, we have a police report to follow up on."

The report was about a girl named Robyn, who was in Grade 5 at Copper's school.

"The police went to Robyn's house over the weekend to check on her because she posted public messages about how sad she was." Copper gathered up her paperwork, and we left her office. I was going to help my first student!

We walked to Robyn's classroom. All the students were spread out around the room reading books except Robyn, who was quietly sitting by herself on a colourful rug at the back of the room. Robyn's book was closed on the floor next to her. She looked lonely and had her arms wrapped around her knees.

Copper stayed at the front of the class to speak to the teacher while I introduced myself to Robyn. I sat down beside her.

Robyn read my vest aloud, "Therapy dog in training." Then she petted me very gently.

I offered Robyn my paw to shake to let her know that I was there to help her. Her tiny hand shook my paw delicately.

Robyn said she didn't have any friends in her class. She believed that she looked and acted differently than the other students. Then Robyn put her arm around me and showed me her phone. "I spend a lot of time alone on my phone. I posted online about how sad I am."

Usually, a dog would be alarmed at hearing that news. Dogs are highly social animals and make friends quickly, especially at the dog park. Most dogs would think it was the same for humans in schools. But not me. I had a secret to share with Robyn. I stood up and tilted my head to the side, and patiently waited for her to finish.

Robyn stared down at her phone. "The police were called to my house to check on me because of the depressing messages I posted. I think that's why Constable Val brought you to see me."

Robyn said she didn't mean to scare anyone, but she had felt alone and couldn't think of a way to feel better.

I told Robyn, "I understand. I used to feel the same way."

Robyn sat up straighter and leaned toward me to listen to my story.

"I'm brown and white and look very different from my dog family, who are all black and white. Also, they're hyperactive, and I'm calm and quiet. It's hard, looking and acting differently."

"We sound very similar, Hershey. Do you think you could help me find some friends?" Robyn looked hopeful.

I was lost for words. I knew I was a good listener, but I wanted to do more than just listen. I wanted to *really help* kids. But it was almost lunchtime, and I had no idea how to help Robyn find friends. Being a therapy dog was a bigger challenge than I'd thought. I probably should have listened to Hershey Senior.

How could I help humans when I was just a herding dog?

★
CHAPTER 11
A Lesson from Hershey Senior

Copper took me outside for a pee break. Working in the city made me realize I had to schedule bathroom breaks now. I wasn't working on a farm where I had the benefit of lifting my leg on a tree or fence post whenever I wanted.

We went back to Copper's office for lunch. She spoke from experience. "It's really important we let Robyn know that she isn't in any trouble. The only reason the police went to her house was to make sure she was safe. I've been asked to follow-up with Robyn so she can get the help she needs. How do you feel after meeting her?"

I sadly woofed, "I don't know how to help her."

"You'll help her just by being you." Copper's confidence in me was unwavering.

I lay on my new dog bed and thought about Robyn. The lunch hour was slowly ticking by. Some of my herding lessons drifted into my mind. Suddenly, I bolted upright and lifted my ears high in the air with an idea. Copper was right. I knew how to help Robyn! All I needed to do was show her the path I was already on – in herding style.

I sniffed inside Copper's animal therapy bag and grabbed my flying saucer with my teeth. I tugged on my leash so we could return to Robyn's classroom quickly. I hoped she would like my idea.

Class had resumed after lunch, so we asked the teacher if Robyn could be excused. Robyn glanced at Copper and looked worried as she joined us in the hallway. I finally saw what Copper had experienced all those times with kids who were afraid to talk to her.

I asked Robyn if she would like to go outside for a game of fetch so we could continue our earlier discussion. She seemed relieved and quickly agreed.

As we walked, I told Robyn what my dog father, Hershey Senior, had taught me. "As a herding dog, you often have to think while you're running. It's good; movement helps you to think better."

"Ok, Hershey. I trust you," Robyn said and smiled at me.

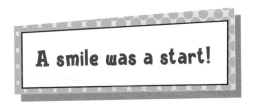

A smile was a start!

Once outside, a few teachers approached Copper to say hi, so I took the opportunity to speak with Robyn some more. I dropped my flying saucer at her feet.

I asked her, "Have you ever seen a border collie therapy dog before? Most service dogs are Labradors or golden retrievers."

"I thought border collies usually work on farms, herding sheep." She threw my flying saucer gently for me to catch and bring back to her.

"You're right," I said, "but I embraced my dream of being different by helping children instead of working on a sheep farm."

Robyn feared, "I'm too different from the students in my class. I don't fit in with anyone."

I happily explained my situation. "Some of my herding dog family judge me for becoming a police therapy dog. Follow your own dreams, Robyn. That's what I'm doing, and it feels GREAT!"

I backed up so she could throw my flying saucer a longer distance. I jumped up high to catch it.

Robyn cheered, "Wow, great catch, Hershey!"

I detected a slight increase in this human's happiness.

After Copper had spoken to the teachers, she joined us by intercepting a throw. Now that my police mom was with us, Robyn looked nervous again. I hoped that she didn't think she was in trouble.

"Nice catch, Constable Val," Robyn said nervously.

"Thanks, Robyn." Copper gave her a warm smile and threw my flying saucer back to her.

I wanted to show Robyn one of my best tricks to help her feel more comfortable around my police mom. I hoped this would make Robyn feel safe enough to open up to Copper and get the help she needed.

When it was my turn to catch, I stood close to a schoolyard bench. Robyn threw my saucer toward me. I jumped up onto the bench and sprang really high into the air. I caught my saucer at the height of my jump and made a perfect landing. This was my best catching trick.

"Cool trick, Hershey!" Robyn giggled and clapped.

I dropped my saucer at Copper's feet.

Copper threw my saucer at Robyn, who caught it easily and confidently.

"You have terrific throwing and catching skills," Copper complimented Robyn.

"Thank you, Constable Val," Robyn murmured while looking at the ground.

I could tell that Robyn was relieved the question wasn't about the police going to her house.

Then Copper reassured Robyn that she wasn't in any trouble and that we were there to help. Copper asked Robyn what some of her interests were.

"I like fashion," she said. Although she spoke quietly, I was relieved she was at least communicating with Copper.

Copper had spoken to Robyn's family and teacher, so she had prepared some suggestions to help Robyn.

"I know of an agency that organizes free fashion shows for young girls to participate in."

Robyn perked up. "Really? That sounds really cool, Constable Val."

Copper encouraged Robyn by saying, "With some fun stage experiences, you could become more confident around your peers."

I woofed with excitement. "I embrace my differences, Robyn. Now you can too!"

"If you are interested," Copper continued, "I think your throwing and catching skills would be appreciated by our school's baseball team."

"I've never tried baseball," Robyn responded, who couldn't hold back a smile when she threw my saucer to Copper with ease.

I cheered her on by barking, "I think you would be a terrific baseball player!'

Copper then threw my saucer really fast in my direction to test my catching skills. I swiftly nabbed it out of the air.

"Nice catch, as usual, Hershey," Copper beamed.

"Nothing gets by a border collie," I bragged, wagging my tail high in the air.

Robyn smiled at Copper. "You and Hershey make a great team. I see you have a lot of fun together."

Copper thanked Robyn. "I'm glad my furry partner suggested we come out to the field and play. We did some great brainstorming today." We all high-fived.

I guess I did learn a thing or two in my herding field after all, as I thought about some of my 'boring' herding lessons.

Then Copper asked me to play dead, followed by a few more tricks of mine. I could tell that Copper and I had eased Robyn's fears about talking to a police officer.

Before we walked Robyn back to her class, she posted some photos of us playing together, and she looked very happy. Copper let Robyn know that the school counsellor would also be following up with her and Robyn was grateful.

I gave her a final piece of advice, "If you get frustrated, you should spend some quality time chewing on a good bone."

Robyn laughed and said she had enough tips for now, then she hugged me and said how much she appreciated the suggestion. I knew she was past the point of gnawing out strategies and was ready to take a bite out of life.

Copper and I ended the day at the cop shop. Sergeant Smith was pleased to hear the successful update about Robyn.

A few of Copper's squadmates petted me as they told funny stories to one another. They had changed out of their police uniforms and were in their civilian clothes. They looked like ordinary humans.

It seemed like Copper was right about one thing. Police officers are regular people who want to help other people – just like I do. I curled up under Copper's desk and sighed out a long breath. I laid my chin on her police boot while she typed up the day's progress report to Inspector Dan.

I was looking forward to going home and putting my paws up.

★
CHAPTER 12
Never Bite when a Good Bark will do

On Wednesday, I woke up before Copper's alarm clock went off. I jumped on her bed, stood over her head, and stared at her until she opened her eyes. I couldn't wait to get to her work. Plus, it was good fun seeing the startled look on her face when she saw my snout hovering over her. Copper's squad was always pulling jokes on each other, and they suggested I do something similar to Copper. I'd have a good story to tell them later.

As we drove to Copper's work, she announced, "We'll go straight to my school again today, Hershey, so you can relax." She giggled.

I breathed only a slight sigh of relief, contrary to the giant one I felt yesterday. I was looking forward to telling Copper's squad my funny story. "Are those police uniforms beginning to grow on me?" I wondered.

When we arrived at Copper's school office, a note was taped to her door. She unlocked her door and read the note while setting our lunches down on her desk. The note was from the school counsellor asking if we could meet with her about a student who needed our help.

While Copper was reading the note out loud, I was sniffing at some cute drawings of me and Copper that had been slipped under the door by a few students.

Copper and I smiled at each other, both thinking that we were already starting to make a difference.

Copper and I walked down the hall to the school counsellor's office. We were introduced to Johnny, a Grade 6 boy. While Copper spoke with the counsellor, Johnny told me that he was in trouble for starting a fight with another student named Megah (MEE-guh). Johnny whispered the whole story to me.

"Megah was trying to climb onto the school's roof, and when I saw him, he dared me to do it too. When I refused, he called me a coward."

Johnny said he didn't like being called a name and felt like he needed to defend his honour, so he started a fist fight with Megah.

"I'm afraid of talking to Constable Val and what will happen to me," said Johnny, his voice trembling. "There's a meeting later this morning with the principal, Constable Val, Megah and me."

I could imagine how Johnny felt. I'd been afraid of police uniforms when I wasn't even in trouble. Johnny must have been terrified.

I thought back to when I accidentally peed on the floor at the animal therapy school. I had found it easier to talk to Copper about my mistake when she had taken me outside. I had been glad I didn't have to explain myself while shamefully staring at a puddle of pee on the floor. I'd needed some distance from the scene of the crime.

I asked Johnny, "Would you like to go outside to the playground?" I hoped that distancing ourselves from the school, and some playtime with Copper and me, might help him feel comfortable with my police mom, like it had for Robyn.

Like a dog who had just been called for dinner, Johnny was up and heading toward the door at once.

Copper had finished speaking with the school counsellor, so I tugged at my leash, which hung on her tool belt. Copper saw Johnny leaving, so she snapped on my leash as I pulled her in Johnny's direction.

In the hallway, my police mom introduced herself to Johnny. The school counsellor had told her what had happened. Copper praised Johnny for not joining Megah in doing a bad thing.

"It takes a lot of inner strength to say 'no'." Copper patted Johnny on the back.

Johnny remained quiet and had his hands in his pockets while we walked to the playground.

Copper was familiar with kids who were too worried to talk to her.

She softened her voice and smiled down at me. "Johnny, would you like to hear how Hershey learned to herd sheep?"

Johnny looked up, slightly curious, in Copper's direction but kept his hands in his pockets.

"When a sheep tries to stray from the flock, it's a herding dog's job to encourage the sheep to fall back in line without hurting the animal."

I knew, of course, exactly what my police mom was trying to teach Johnny.

Then I chimed in, **"Never bite when a good bark will do."**

"Precisely. We can learn a lot from our furry friends." Copper then allowed silence to take over.

We arrived at the playground, and all slid down the slide a few times to ease the tension. Then we continued the herding lesson so Johnny could compare it to his situation.

Copper sat on a swing and stepped backward in the sand to get some height before she started swinging. "Hershey always remained calm when a sheep tried to stray from the flock. In your case, Johnny, when Megah encouraged you to join him in doing a bad thing, you could have said no in the same way that Hershey barked at a wayward sheep."

Johnny finally looked at Copper. "I know. I lost my cool when Megah called me a coward."

Copper jumped off her swing at the top of her height. Her body stumbled during her landing, but surprisingly she stayed on her feet. Johnny kept a laugh to himself.

Copper turned toward Johnny as she brushed some sand off her police pants following the awkward landing. "It can be hard not to react to an insult. If it happens again, verbally take pride in standing up for your values and doing the right thing, instead of physically reacting to being called a name."

Johnny walked over to where Copper was standing. "I had an opportunity to walk away and tell the principal what was going on. Instead, I chose to defend myself physically. Next time I will say 'no' and walk away. Sometimes I don't make good decisions." Johnny looked down at his forearm, where he brushed his fingers over a few scrapes that had resulted from the fight he started with Megah.

Copper thanked Johnny for being honest. Then she lightened the topic. "What do you like to do in your spare time, Johnny?"

"Sometimes I get really bored. I'd like to do more, but I don't have many friends. I've always wanted to learn how to build things out of wood."

"You can mention that to the principal when we're in the meeting today. We're here to help." Copper patted Johnny on the shoulder. Johnny offered a small smile and nodded.

"You could start by building an **addition to my doghouse,**" I suggested.

We all laughed.

As we entered the school's main doors, Johnny announced, "I'm ready to go to the meeting now."

But when Johnny looked in the office window, he saw two of Megah's friends in the principal's office with Megah. Johnny spun around and yelled at me.

"You set me up, Hershey! Megah's friends are in there, and they'll gang up on me! I should never have trusted a police dog. You're a terrible therapy dog. Don't ever talk to me again!" Johnny ran down the hall and out of sight.

I was devastated.

Copper yelled something to Johnny. I heard the words "misunderstanding" and "come back" but Johnny was gone. I lay down at Copper's police boots, closed my eyes, and in my mind, I agreed with Johnny. I was a terrible therapy dog. Copper wouldn't have any progress to report to Sergeant Smith or Inspector Dan about my work this morning. In fact, I'd probably made things worse.

I whimpered.

"I'm going to call Hershey Senior and tell him that I'll come work for him."

★
CHAPTER 13
Herding comes in Handy

It was lunchtime, but I had no appetite. I snuck away from Copper and tracked the scent of Johnny's footprints back to the playground where we'd just had that great discussion. I was confused about how it had gone so wrong, so fast.

"Hershey!" Copper came running over to me, out of breath. "There you are. I'm sorry for what Johnny yelled at you."

I was so upset that I covered my eyes with my paws and told myself I had bitten off more than I could chew with this career. I knew if I looked into Copper's eyes, I would cry. I was also mad at her. Why hadn't she told me that Megah's friends were going to gang up on Johnny?

Copper's tone was apologetic. "I'm sorry I didn't tell you ahead of time that Megah's friends would be at the meeting."

I stood up and howled, "Johnny said those boys are going to gang up on him!"

"Just the opposite, Hershey," Copper soothed. "Megah's friends are there to support both Megah and Johnny."

I sat down, even more confused now. "Why would they do that?"

"Megah's friends don't like what Megah was trying to do, and they want him to get some help. They want to share some positive stories about Megah's good character. This way, the principal and I will have a balanced view about him."

Copper's knees made cracking noises as she slowly squatted down in front of me. She petted my head. "Johnny was informed that he could also bring supporters, but he said he didn't have any. Do you think you can encourage Johnny to return to the office and be his supporter?"

I loved how my police mom's eyebrows lifted and smushed together when she really hoped an idea would work. She also put her hands together like she was praying. Copper had done a good job apologizing, but she could tell I was still upset.

"I don't want Johnny and Megah to have a written police record because of their poor choices. I want to take a verbal, restorative approach to resolve this."

I stumbled over the word. "Ree-stor-a-tiv?"

"Yes. A restorative approach is based on respect and compassion. If we can gather everyone affected by this incident together and let everyone have a turn to talk, we'll have a good idea of everyone's needs."

I liked what Copper was saying. I appreciate when people ask me how I feel when I make a mistake. It helps me own up to my poor decisions if I can tell my side of the story.

"Hershey, if you can bring Megah and Johnny together, it'll give them, and the rest of us, an opportunity to repair the harm that has been done."

"So, are you saying that **communication helps repair harm?**" I perked my ears up a little bit.

"Yes! It sounds like you have a good understanding of restorative justice already." Copper smiled.

Border Collies are fast learners. I stood up and accepted Copper's apology by giving her an extra-slobbery Hershey kiss on her cheek.

"Do you think your superpower nose can find Johnny?"

"Woof!" I happily accepted the challenge.

Now that the misunderstanding was cleared up, I jumped off Copper's lap, shook off my self-pity and set off to find Johnny. It was still lunchtime, and I'd have to stay focused and not be distracted by tasty aromas in the hallways. The office staff had paged Johnny over the intercom to return to the office, but I knew we had lost his trust.

Many students tried to pet me in the crowded hallways, so I had to rely on my herding skills. I was able to move large numbers of students to the side so that I could run through the hallways quickly. The longer Johnny was mad at me, the smaller my chances were of encouraging him to come to the meeting.

I suspected that Johnny wanted to be alone, so I searched for students seated by themselves. My canine senses were on high alert. I did, however, have the misfortune of smelling many sweaty running shoes and lockers containing mouldy lunches.

Finally, I saw Johnny sitting down and leaning against a locker at the end of the last hall. The expression on his face was very sad. It looked like I was too late.

As I slowly approached Johnny, I could smell fear on him. I got closer and saw tears of disappointment streaming down his face.

"Go away," Johnny snarled at me. "I don't even like dogs."

I crawled toward his feet. I apologetically wedged my nose under his elbow.

I heard someone run up behind me. It was Copper. I hadn't realized that she'd done such a good job keeping up with me.

"Johnny," Copper panted, "I want to explain why Megah's friends are in the meeting."

Johnny just stared down at his half-eaten sandwich.

Copper spoke while trying to catch her breath, "Megah's friends want to thank you for helping him."

"Thank me? For *helping* him?" Johnny looked halfway up at Copper with a bewildered expression.

Copper nodded and looked relieved. "Megah's friends called me when they saw you trying to stop him from climbing onto the school roof. They had tried to stop Megah before, but he had refused to listen."

Johnny looked up fully at Copper.

Copper then smiled. "Megah's friends were really impressed that you stood up for your school. They would like to see you get some advice about a safer way of standing up for yourself."

I wagged my tail, but I have to admit, I was holding back tears. I gave Johnny a Hershey kiss on his hand and was tremendously relieved when he responded by petting my head.

Making up after a disagreement as soon as possible is of the utmost importance in the dog world.

It is in the human world too, but it can take longer for some humans.

I then expressed, "Johnny, I apologize." I quickly gave his hand multiple Hershey kisses. "I didn't know Megah's friends had been invited to the meeting. Otherwise, I would have given you the heads-up. I'm new to being a police therapy dog. I'm still training to do the job. I understand how hurt you must feel."

Johnny leaned over and surprised me with a long hug. "Apology accepted, Hershey, but only if you accept mine too. I love doggos – especially you. You're an awesome police therapy dog. You're *pawsome!*"

Johnny and I both laughed, and I sighed a huge breath of relief.

Johnny stood up and apologized to Copper for running off. "If it's not too late to attend the meeting... ."

Copper kindly interrupted Johnny. "It's never too late. I'm the one who needs to apologize for not telling you and my furry partner that Megah's friends were going to be there." They both smiled, and she patted Johnny on the back.

Feeling relieved, we walked back to the office together.

During the meeting, Johnny and Megah each took responsibility for their actions. They offered to do community service hours to make up for the incident. Apologies were made, handshakes were exchanged, and hurt feelings were mended.

Copper said that she would help Johnny find a carpentry class. When Megah asked if he and his friends could join the class, Johnny was delighted! He was happy that he made new friends out of a difficult situation. It was a successful meeting.

To my surprise, the principal (who I believed wasn't a dog person) picked me up and squeezed me so tight I thought I might fart. "I'm so happy you're helping us in our school, Hershey! I'll give Inspector Dan an outstanding rating about you today."

Johnny walked over to me after Megah and his friends had left.

"I appreciate all of your support, Hershey. Constable Val is really cool after all," he said confidently. Then he smiled and asked to shake my paw.

I was happy for Johnny. I told him that my friend, Smooch, suggested I learn a funny trick for the kids I'd be working with. "This one is called 'Hide from the cops'." I lay down and covered my eyes with my paws.

Johnny laughed. "Really funny trick, Hershey!"

Copper and I ended our day in her school office. She opened her bottom desk drawer for me to help myself to my dog cookies while she typed up today's progress report for Inspector Dan.

That night at home, I dropped heavily onto my dog bed and realized how challenging but also rewarding Copper's job as a police officer was. I wondered who I could help tomorrow.

One thing was for sure; training to be a police therapy dog was keeping me on my paws.

★ CHAPTER 14

Sniffing out my own Case

Thursday was my last day to prove myself to Inspector Dan. On our drive in, Copper had said that Friday would be an office day at the police station, and we wouldn't be working with any kids. I had to make Thursday count. I really wanted Inspector Dan to hire me to keep working with Copper and the kids in her school. Today, the pressure was on.

We started our workday in the bullpen at the cop shop. Inspector Dan had told Copper that he still wasn't impressed with me and said I had been lucky the past three days. He said I hadn't solved a case on my own yet, from start to finish.

"What's a case?" I asked Copper.

She explained enthusiastically, "It's a thorough investigation the police do when a crime happens. The police talk to everyone involved until they all get the help they need."

Looking back, I guess I was introduced to students whose cases were already started.

Copper reassured me. "You're doing great, Hershey. Keep up the good work, and you'll sniff out a case on your own. Trust those incredible canine instincts of yours."

I was more than ready. Border collies thrive under pressure.

While Copper checked her emails, I trotted into Sergeant Smith's office and gave him a high five. I told him about the prank I pulled on Copper the previous morning. He laughed and threw a dog cookie high in the air to reward me. I skillfully caught it and wagged my tail on the way out to thank him for the treat. I carried the cookie in my teeth back to Copper's desk, where I enjoyed my first treat of the day. I was so glad I worked past my fear of people in police uniforms. Cops are cool!

Once Copper was all caught up on her station work, we drove to her school.

That morning, the girls' gym teacher jogged into Copper's office. The teacher looked quite athletic. I thought she would be very successful running in a field, herding sheep. She sat down in the chair closest to my box of dog cookies, reached into the box and offered me one as she asked for our help. While I devoured my second treat of the day, I listened attentively to her.

"Some of my students have had a few of their personal items go missing. It seems to happen in the morning during the Grade 9 girls' yoga class. There have also been some disappearances at lunch hour during the Grade 7 girls' soccer intramurals."

I sat up and offered her my paw to shake.

Copper read my mind. "I think Hershey is offering some *pawsitive* police assistance."

The teacher smiled and reached out her muscular arm to accept my paw shake. I told her that her case was in good paws. She thanked us for any help we could provide and then jogged out of Copper's office.

This would be my first case to solve from start to finish! I would prove to Inspector Dan that I was valuable in his unit. Surely he'd hire me if I investigated this case all on my own!

Copper and I set out right away for the yoga class. I didn't want to waste one minute.

"I see you're sniffing the air, Hershey. Your nose is 50 times more powerful than a human's. What do you smell?"

My brain is also 40 times greater at analyzing smells than human brains.

The girls had started warming up, so I walked around, alert for anything suspicious. I was relying on my natural ability to read body language and emotion, but I didn't smell anything unusual. I couldn't leave without helping the girls with their up-dog and down-dog poses.

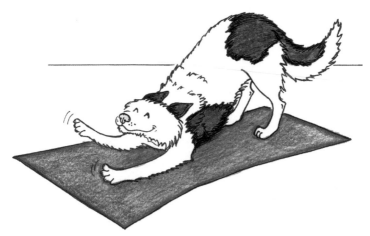

Copper and I returned for the Grade 7 intramural soccer game at lunchtime to continue our case. I herded the girls together, like a good border collie, and offered a few pawshakes. The girls invited me to play as a goalie, my specialty. This was a great introduction that allowed me to get to know them better. Of course, I was undefeatable on the net, but I did have twice as many legs as they did.

After the game, Copper spoke to the gym teacher while one of the girls came up to me. She was the goalie I had played against.

"Congratulations on your shutout, Hershey." The girl wiped her shirt sleeve on her sweaty forehead.

My mind was on my case, so I took a long sniff of her while I thanked her for the compliment. I didn't detect any fear scent, which means she smelled normal, like the other girls I had pressed my nose against.

"If you want to improve your soccer skills," I suggested, **"you should try herding sheep."**

She laughed, patted my head and sat down with her friends. Her body language wasn't out of the ordinary, so I eliminated her as a suspect.

A few minutes before the girls left for their next class, Copper and I spoke to the teams about the missing property. She informed them that we would be staying in the gym if anyone wanted to come forward with information.

When Copper was done speaking, she walked back to the gym teacher. I took this time to show the remaining girls a few of my tricks. I thought this distance from my police mom would help someone confide in me – and it worked! All the girls went to their next class, with one exception.

As that girl kneeled beside me, I sensed right away through her body language and expression that something was wrong.

"Hi, Hershey," she said almost soundlessly.

"Hello," I softly responded. I gave her hand a Hershey kiss and sensed she needed to tell me something.

"It was me who took the items from the girls' locker room, but please don't tell Constable Val."

As my nose detected the scent of fear, I thought, "I can't keep a secret from Copper."

I had an overwhelming feeling of compassion for this sorrowful student. She was reluctant to tell me her name, so I gave her my best puppy dog eyes and promised her that I was there to help her.

"Aww, you're so sweet, Hershey. I'm Roxanne." She petted me over and over.

I sat down beside her to continue the connection we had started.

"Thank you for your bravery and honesty." I leaned in closer to her. "It takes a lot of courage to talk about our mistakes, but we all make them."

I first thought of doing some tricks for Roxanne to cheer her up, but instead, my doggie instincts guided me to tell her a story about when I had made a mistake.

"At home on my farm, I'm not allowed in the vegetable garden. One day, when I was a puppy, I felt rebellious and wanted to take the neighbour's dog bone that was lying just beyond our fence."

Roxanne kept petting me slowly as I continued to tell my story. "To get the bone, I had to cross the forbidden vegetable garden. As soon as I went in, I sank deep into the dirt. I hadn't realized that my mom had just watered the garden, so it was very muddy. I poked my head under the fence and took the bone in my teeth. When I came out of the garden, I had mud all over my legs, tummy and tail."

"What happened next, Hershey?" Roxanne asked with a concerned look on her face and tenderness in her voice.

"When my mom saw me, she was mad. I cowered in fear. She yelled something about vegetable seeds and that the garden was ruined. I felt terrible. She washed the mud off me with the garden hose and threw the bone in the garbage. I felt awful for taking it, and I couldn't even return it. I apologized to my mom with my best Hershey kisses. She forgave me and said we all make mistakes."

Copper then walked over to us. She slowly sat down on the floor beside us, wincing as she struggled to adjust her police gear and get comfortable.

Once settled in, Copper noticed right away that Roxanne looked reluctant to engage with her. My attentive police mom kept the subject light. She asked Roxanne if she was hungry now that her soccer match was over.

The quiet student kept her gaze toward the floor and nodded.

Copper suggested that Roxanne have lunch and then go to her next class.

Roxanne slowly stood up, patted my head goodbye and walked out of the gymnasium with her head hung low.

My head was also hanging low because Roxanne asked me to keep a secret from Copper.

Copper and I stood up and walked down the hallway, returning to our office to eat lunch.

My police mom sighed. "I guess by Roxanne's body language that she's responsible for the thefts."

Copper was a trained investigator. She already knew what Roxanne wasn't telling her.

"This is your case, Hershey. What do you think Roxanne needs from us?"

I didn't have an answer for Copper, but I was grateful she didn't ask me if Roxanne had confessed. I wanted to respect Roxanne's wishes and not tell my police mom that she had confided in me.

I stared at the ham sandwich Copper had packed for my lunch but couldn't eat. I walked over to my dog bed, turned around three times, and lay down. I thought I might have been over my soft, silky head in this job. Being a police therapy dog was a big responsibility.

I felt like I was barking up the wrong tree with this career. If I couldn't solve that case, then maybe I wouldn't get hired by Inspector Dan after all.

★
CHAPTER 15
Horsing around Helps

I could hear Copper crunching on the dreadful greens she had brought for lunch. She had once tried feeding me spinach scraps after dinner, and I'd instantly sneezed all over them.

"A salad a day keeps the doctor away, Hershey," she sensibly stated.

I shuddered. I turned my thoughts to how I could help Roxanne. I hoped I could come up with a solution, but the answer was still a mystery to me. I sighed.

After lunch, when the hallway was quiet, Copper and I asked Roxanne's teacher if she could be excused from class. Roxanne sat down next to me on the hallway floor. Copper creaked and groaned her way onto the floor beside us. Roxanne didn't appear nervous around my police mom, as Robyn and Johnny had been; Roxanne was withdrawn.

My superior doggie senses told me that the quiet girl had a lot she wanted to say but couldn't say it.

Roxanne leaned over, patted me sweetly, and spoke affectionately. "I really love animals. I wish I could be around them all the time."

That was it! I asked Copper, "Can we call Molly?"

I explained to Roxanne, "Molly is a friend of mine who's a therapy horse."

"A horrrrrse?" Roxanne smiled and looked like she had just been granted a wish. She sat up very straight.

My police mom knew from Roxanne's reaction that it was a great suggestion.

> **"A horse can be a strong source of support,"** Copper explained.

I told Roxanne, "I learned in animal therapy school that *any* animal could help people." I stood up and wagged my tail.

Roxanne also stood up and had flushed cheeks at the possibility of having a live visit with a horse. "I've never actually petted a horse before, but I love them."

My police mom stood up faster than usual, then pulled out her phone and dialled. I was learning from Copper that the police wanted to understand *why* people broke the law to help prevent it from happening again. If Molly could help Roxanne open up to Copper and confess about the items she took, then Copper could get Roxanne the help she needed.

While Copper called Molly's owner, Roxanne crossed her arms tightly together. She bounced slightly on her heels, doing her best at holding back a hopeful smile. It was clear to me that Roxanne craved animals in her life. Molly seemed to be the perfect solution to help Roxanne open up. I felt like a general doctor referring a patient to a specialist.

Copper hung up, clasped her hands together, and raised her eyebrows. She happily told Roxanne that Molly had an immediate opening.

"Yes!" Roxanne exhaled loudly as if she'd been holding her breath the entire length of the phone call.

Soon after the permission forms were completed, we drove to our city's equestrian centre, located in the river valley. Molly's stable was a facility that was open to the public, and there were horses and riders everywhere.

"Look at all the horses!" Roxanne exclaimed with joy. "I love it!" She ran straight to the riding arena, where Molly and the instructor were waiting for us.

By the time Copper and I caught up with Roxanne, she was already on Molly's back. Roxanne smiled and lay down on her tummy, giving Molly a big hug. Then she rested her chin on the back of her hands as though she had been born on a horse. Roxanne seemed like a different girl. When she glanced down at me, she had a huge smile and a lot of love in her eyes. I felt pride in that look.

Roxanne said she had always wanted to be around animals but had never had the opportunity. She sat up, let out a big sigh and opened up to Copper. "It was me who stole from the girls' locker room."

"Thank you, Roxanne. Do you want to share with us why you took the items?" asked Copper, who was standing beside Molly, petting her head.

Roxanne's voice quivered with regret. "I thought it would make me happy to have things that I don't have. But it didn't. Thanks to my new friend, Hershey, I realize how important being around animals and nature is to me. This is what brings me joy. I knew it was wrong to steal. I will return all the items. I'm truly sorry. It won't happen again."

"Thank you for your openness, Roxanne. People do have to find what brings them joy." Copper bent down to pet me. "Thanks to my furry and intuitive partner who helped Roxanne talk about her mistakes and find happiness."

"I love Molly!" Roxanne leaned forward onto her tummy again, giving my Percheron horse friend another big squeeze. "Do you think I could see this big loveable girl again? Could I be a volunteer here?"

Copper turned toward the instructor. "Do you need some help caring for Molly?"

The instructor gave a great big sigh of relief. "I could really use an extra set of hands around here."

"Thank you!" Roxanne squeaked as she sat up and squirmed on Molly's back.

Roxanne shared with Copper that she was Indigenous.

"Roxanne, did you know that horses are a traditional First Nations icon? The bond that Indigenous people have with horses is an important aspect of their history."

"I'd love to learn more about my ancestral culture." Roxanne's eyes widened with curiosity.

The instructor was of Métis heritage, and she was kind. She stepped forward to pet Molly's velvety nose and said to Roxanne, "If you like, I could share some of the Indigenous teachings I've been given."

Roxanne quickly accepted her offer and thanked her.

Copper then brought the conversation back to the thefts. "Roxanne, we need to conclude our case with everyone involved in the thefts of the girls' property. Would you be willing to participate in a restorative justice circle?"

"What's that?" Roxanne looked worried.

"A restorative justice circle is a gathering of everyone to resolve conflict. I embrace traditional Indigenous views of justice, and I'm a certified restorative justice facilitator. I could lead a circle if you wanted."

"Does this mean that I'm still in trouble, even if I give back the items?" Roxanne leaned down again, giving Molly a hug for support.

My police mom explained, "Roxanne, restorative justice practices don't focus on blame and punishment when people make mistakes."

Roxanne sat up, looking relieved. "Okay," said Roxanne, still looking a little unsure of what Copper had said.

"Participation in a circle can build understanding and closure for everyone." Copper petted Molly's nose.

Roxanne lifted her arms out to the side and let them flop against her legs. "I feel like I can talk about anything out here! I can help everyone understand what I did if I can talk with Molly and Hershey present. Could the circle be out here with Molly?" Roxanne inquired with hope in her voice.

Copper turned to the instructor again and answered before Copper could ask anything.

"I'd be honoured to host your circle here with our horses."

"Thank you!" Roxanne smiled while petting Molly.

Copper then explained to Roxanne that everyone who attended the circle would be offered a horse for support. Each person would be given an equal opportunity to speak and be listened to.

> **What a very large and reassuring circle,** I thought to myself.

Copper continued, "Roxanne, it'll be a great start to repairing the relationships that have been damaged. At the end of the circle, we can help you create healing through accountability."

"What does that mean?" Roxanne kept petting her beautiful support horse for reassurance.

"When we make mistakes, it's important to be accountable for them. You've already volunteered to help with Molly. Those hours can account for you taking responsibility for the thefts."

"I'm happy to take responsibility for what I did," said Roxanne, sounding motivated.

"It won't all be grooming and riding," the instructor said with a friendly laugh. "There'll be a lot of horse droppings that need to be shovelled to the manure pile."

"No problem," answered Roxanne, also laughing. "Anything that beautiful Molly needs, I can help with!"

Roxane dismounted and gave Molly one last hug. Then she turned toward us. "I haven't wanted to talk to anyone for a long time about how unhappy I've been. Thanks for caring so much about my side of the story."

"I've been teaching my police mom a thing or two this week," I ruffed.

Everyone laughed, including Molly.

We all walked back to Copper's police vehicle feeling uplifted. Roxanne was in the right hands, paws, and hooves.

Later that evening, I was curled up on my dog bed in the living room at home. I thought back to the very beginning, when Copper had said that some kids were too afraid to talk to her.

In the kitchen, I overheard Copper talking to my human dad. "Roxanne may never have received the help she needed without the work of my furry partner today."

"Furry and charming," I woofed toward the kitchen.

"*Very* charming," Copper hollered back.

I stretched out my legs with a long, loud sigh. I reflected on the kids I had helped that week. I hoped our good work proved to Inspector Dan that I was the perfect partner for Copper.

I tossed and turned in my sleep until Copper's alarm clock went off.

★
CHAPTER 16
Feels like Seven

Friday morning, I sprang out of bed. I dashed in and out of every room in the house, barking loudly. My family knew that Inspector Dan was making his decision that day. I was hoping to be an official Compassion Bodyguard!

Copper sat down on the floor to groom me. "We got this, Hershey! This is what we've both been hoping for."

I was too full of beans to eat breakfast, so Copper packed some snacks to go, and we left the house early. I believed she was as eager as I was, but she was better at containing it.

Before Copper could put her car in park at the cop shop, I rolled down my window, leaped out, and bolted through the front doors. I scanned my ID card and raced straight to Inspector Dan's office, but his door was shut. I sat down and stared through his office window into the dark, motionless office.

My ears drooped with disappointment.

I heard Copper's footsteps approaching.

I whined, "Surely, today is a big day for Inspector Dan, too?

"Don't worry, Hershey," Copper replied calmly as she did her wave thing. "He should be in shortly."

I thought he wanted to hire me in his Youth Unit since he had paid for all of my training and let me come to work with Copper for a week. So, why wasn't he here?

I trailed after Copper towards her desk. She told me that we had a long and important meeting that morning. I asked her if it was about me, but she said it wasn't. I lay down and sighed.

When was Inspector Dan going to arrive and tell us the good news? Maybe it was bad news, and he was delaying telling us? I told myself to think *pawsitively*. I sighed again and tried to redirect my thoughts. I rested my chin on my paw and started daydreaming about what my title would be if I was hired.

Police Pup Hershey had a nice ring to it. Or maybe **Hershey, the Police Therapy Dog.**

"Hershey," Copper interrupted my daydream, "come."

Everyone in the office loved it when they saw me follow Copper to the photocopier or the lunchroom. I even followed her into the bathroom. She always chose the biggest stall so that I could fit too. I'd poke my head under the other stalls and sniff at the ladies' shoes.

I'll never understand why humans don't act more like dogs while in the bathroom. The stalls make it impossible to socialize and discover valuable scent information from one another.

Copper called me to the meeting in the boardroom. Three professionals from different youth agencies entered the room. I met them at the door and herded them to their seats. Herding was still instinctual.

"You sure are a border collie, aren't ya, Hersh?" Copper smiled.

I wagged my tail. I just preferred to herd people instead of sheep.

While the group discussed the kids they were working with, I settled under the table at Copper's feet. I let out an impatient sigh. Where was Inspector Dan? Honestly, sometimes humans take forever to do things.

I've heard that one hour feels like seven for a dog. It was starting to feel like seven indeed.

★
CHAPTER 17
Inspector Dan's Decision

After lunch, Inspector Dan must have sneaked in through the back door of the cop shop, as I hadn't smelled him go by Copper's desk. I had been gnawing on a delicious marrow bone that Copper gave me to help me pass the time. I hadn't noticed how quiet the office had become. Everyone was gone. Inspector Dan startled me when he spoke.

"Hershey, can you follow me, please?"

He looked serious. I was too afraid to ask if I had done something wrong. I followed closely as he briskly headed to the back of the building, where there was a grassy area outside. I hoped this wasn't about my pooing. I thought I had done a good job showing Copper where I had pooped while at work.

When Inspector Dan opened the back door, all the staff were there. They cheered, "Surprise, Hershey! Congratulations!"

Copper ran over to me and put a party hat on my head.

Inspector Dan then asked everyone for their attention.

Was it true? Was Inspector Dan going to hire me?

"I'm pleased to offer Hershey a job as a certified police therapy dog in our Youth Unit.

"Bow-wow-wow!" I yowled. I chased my tail in circles, did some puppy bows, and then sprinted in a big circle around everyone while barking from the rooftops! I couldn't contain my excitement! Inspector Dan hired me!

"Hershey," Inspector Dan called out to me.

I raced back to Inspector Dan and sat down in front of his big belly. I had to hold myself back from giving him a wet Hershey kiss on his plump cheek.

Inspector Dan bent down on one knee in front of me. It was the first time I had seen him smile. I thought you couldn't teach an old person new tricks?

"Mrs. Katz told me that you're the youngest dog to graduate from her animal therapy school. She also reported that your obedience skills were the best she had ever seen. Your school results, combined with an impressive workweek with Constable Val, landed you a thumbs up from me. I'm extremely impressed! Welcome to the Youth Unit." He held out his chunky hand for me to shake.

I rapidly put my paw on his open hand. I've never had a more fulfilling paw-hand shake.

"Welcome *officially* to the team," everyone else chimed in, taking turns petting my head and shaking my paws. "We made your favourite cake to celebrate: peanut butter!"

Sergeant Smith walked over to me, whistling, *'For he's a jolly good fellow.'*

"I knew all along you were *pawfect* for the job, Police Pup. I'm honoured to have you on my team," he said as his strong hand patted me on my back.

If I could have done a backflip, I would have, but all I could do was happily pant and enjoy the moment.

As Sergeant Smith walked away, he called out to me, "Squad run at 0600 hours Monday morning, Police Pup!"

I ruffed back in agreement. I couldn't wait to run circles around Copper's squad.

Copper then came over to me. "Hershey, every dog has his day, and today is yours! I want to thank you for this week. I know it wasn't easy for you. I saw on many occasions how uncomfortable you were, but you did it!" Copper said with a crackly voice.

If I didn't know better, it sounded like my non-emotional police mom was choking up a bit.

Copper continued, "The kids we worked with this week benefited so much from your support and unique ideas. You're the coolest partner I've ever had!"

A few of Copper's squadmates looked surprised and insulted. They shook their heads and whispered to one another while pointing to themselves. "I thought I was the coolest partner she ever had?"

I wrapped my paws around my police mom's neck, and we hugged for a long time.

Copper then gave me a new vest to replace my training vest.

"Certified Police Therapy Dog, Hershey," Copper read aloud.

I did it!

"I also have an announcement for you, Hershey. Smooch has been hired with the RCMP. He is going to be the greeter at the police station."

I was very happy for Smooch! And for anyone who walks into his police station. I'm sure they will love his impressive tricks.

A familiar voice of a guardian angel then spoke. "Congratulations, Hershey," Marley said as she walked up to me. "I have been hearing about your progress all week. I am very proud of you."

I looked up, and Annie was standing next to Copper. Annie leaned down to me and whispered, "It's ok to ask her on a date, Hershey," as she gave me the ok symbol.

I jumped up against Copper and gave her cheek my biggest Hershey kiss ever to thank her for inviting Marley.

I then looked up disappointingly at the fur sticking out on my head. I licked my paw and flattened the unruly pieces. I hoped Marley would be attracted to me now that I had an education and a career. When Marley gave me her number, I felt like a dog with two tails. Extremely happy!

Copper's squad patted me on the back and asked me to join them for a drink at their watering hole. It sounded awful to me, and I hoped it was cleaner than our sheeps' watering hole. I asked them if I could take a raincheck. I was exhausted and wanted to get home to my dog family to share my good news.

Once I got home, I bolted straight to my dog family's farm to tell them my incredible news. "Inspector Dan hired me! I am officially a police therapy dog!"

All of my dog family swarmed me with hugs and kisses.

I thanked Hershey Senior for all he had taught me. I told him how I related his herding lessons to my new career of helping kids. For the first time in my life, my dog father placed his paw on my shoulder and said, "I'm proud of you, son." When he walked over to his bed and laid down, I was certain I saw a crack of a smile on his face.

My dog brother, Aero, had been doing a great job of taking care of our sheep while I had been training to become a police therapy dog.

"Cool gig, bro. You will be a great cop dog." Then Aero asked me if he could permanently take over my herding job on Copper's farm. I told him I would be ecstatic for him to replace me and thanked him for stepping in.

We then had our own party, in herding style. We ran through the fields, chasing each other, and had steak and potatoes for dinner.

After our celebration, and as I trotted home to Copper, I reflected on how exhilarating the past two weeks of my life had been. It was a good thing I could sleep in tomorrow. I was dog-tired. I wondered if Copper would cook her famous rancher's breakfast the next day. Even though she would never admit it in a million dog years, I think she was dog-tired too.

I curled up on my bed. I wondered who I would help next week. Maybe there would be more cookies too.

★
APPENDIX A

A Message from Hershey, Police Therapy Dog

*H*i, friends! It's Hershey here. During my career, I've met many kids who had a lot to say but didn't know how to say it. If you need help, ask to see a therapy dog. A visit with any therapy animal can help you put your feelings and thoughts into words. With a therapy dog's guidance, those words can be the beginning of many conversations to help solve any problem.

Check out my website at
www.hersheythepolicetherapydog.com

★
APPENDIX B
How Animal Therapy Started in the Youth Unit

by Hershey's Police Mom, Copper

Hershey is a seven-year-old border collie and was a certified police therapy dog for four years. The idea to bring animal therapy to the high-risk youth section of our police service began after I learned of a corrections officer who proactively utilized a black Labrador in an adult detention centre.

The lab wagged a solution, in my eyes, to the age-old barrier between troubled youth and police: trust.

Generally speaking, successful interventions with justice-involved youth are not immediate. It takes time to build trust between youth and the police. The presence of a therapy dog speeds up this process significantly. Dogs are intelligent, sensitive and non-judgmental; an open and shut case for helping the police and youth connect. As time goes on, the consistent use of a therapy dog can strengthen relationships between youth and the police and other agencies working with the same youth.

This connection vastly helps the youth persevere in

developing themselves and moving forward in life in a trusting, fun and natural manner. The human-canine service team is like the family the youth may have never had, right down to the family dog.

Encourage professionals in your line of work, at your school, or in your home to use therapy dogs. Also, try to include movement. Policing, social work, teaching, and other professions can be stressful to youth and everyone else involved. With a dog present and an activity, when possible, stress shifts tremendously to something positive and productive.

When kids need a hand, offer them a paw first.

★ ABOUT THE AUTHOR
Val Hoglund

by Hershey

Val, aka 'Copper', has been a police officer for 32 years. When Copper was in the Youth Unit, she learned more about the youth and why they were committing crimes. She wanted to do something *pawsitive* about it. Then I padded in.

I asked Copper some questions about herself:

Hershey: What is your educational background? Do you have obedience training?

Copper: I obediently studied in university for two years, working towards an education degree.

Hershey: Do you have a certification like I do?

Copper: Yes, I am a certified restorative justice facilitator.

Hershey: Cool. My greatest assets are my million-dollar nose and that I'm human's best friend. What do you consider your best assets?

Copper: My dog...

Hershey: That's a great answer

Copper: ...and my high amount of energy.

Hershey: Do you have any goals?

Copper: My goal is to be as wonderful as my dog thinks I am.

★
ABOUT THE ILLUSTRATOR
Liv Vors

Liv is a police officer and is an Edmonton-based illustrator who loves animals, naps and coffee. She hails from northeastern Saskatchewan and has been drawing ever since she was old enough to hold a crayon. Prior to policing, Liv worked in wildlife biology and was a nationally published food writer.

Her web cartoon on Instagram
@thinbluescribble
shows the lighter side of law enforcement.

★ ABOUT THE NARRATOR

by Hershey

This is my official portrait. It was created by DanSun Photos. Thanks, Dan Sundahl. You rock!

I love going out for nice long runs with Copper in the countryside, but my favourite pastime is a good ol' game of ball.

I'm an exception to the traditionally hyperactive border collie. Copper tells people that I think I'm a cat. I'm just the strong and silent type.

I love my house buddy, Frankie, the cat. I herd Frankie around the yard when Copper is gardening, and from room to room if she's in the house. A Border collie never goes off-duty.

My best friend is a bernadoodle named Moose.

Many people ask Copper if I'm a girl and her response is always the same, "No, he's a boy. He just looks pretty."

When regular dogs see me in my working vest, I wonder if they think, "Oh no, it's a cop."

I love bacon. Plus, I also like to be fed burgers, pork chops, and steak. I'm worth it.

And I don't like baths. Or swimming.

★
HERSHEY WOULD
LIKE TO THANK

by Hershey

My family for their patience and support for this book over the past four years. I love you furry much!

The Edmonton Police Association and the Edmonton Community Foundation (Good luck in retirement, Martin!) for their generous support of this book.

Peter and Heather for teaching my police mom how to listen. It *is* all about relationships!

The insightful Dan, who trusted me to begin my therapy work without hesitation. Those successful interventions were our desired outcome.

Charlie's Angels for all the encouragement, referrals, laughs, brainstorming, fun road trips, activities, and unending friendship. I love you guys!

My supportive surveillance squad for believing in this intervention. Thanks for your patience with my dog hair in the vehicles, the cookies in your desks, the funny nicknames (like *Hershey Squirts*), and the referrals for your youth.

The Laura's and Leeanne, who made it feel like the office was a playground, and for reminding Copper about the human side of policing. (I taught her not to judge.)

Lawrence and Em for allowing me to take my time in our friendship and for years of ball throwing in the halls. I loved it!

Michelle and Greg for recognizing me in the highlights, for the peanut butter, and all the second chances, especially when I was growly at uniforms or new male visitors to our office.

An enormous thank you to all the agencies that never blinked twice about allowing me to work in your buildings with your employees and your youth. I couldn't have done my good work without your constant support.

My editors, Jaimie Hoglund and Bryony van der Merwe, for making this book possible: you get me and Copper!

Gary Millar, for all the help you gave Copper's youth, the coffee dates and encouragement for this book...all for free! You are a gift, and we treasure you.

Sherwood School (now Alex Janvier school) and Bessie Nichols School for being my first live audience. Your feedback was appreciated, and we had so much fun! Stay well and know that the police, and therapy animals, are always your friends.

Our friends and overseas loved ones for all your contributions and patience in helping see this book to the end.

Liv would like to thank her parents, Norma and Uffe, for always encouraging her to be creative. Her police family is always an endless source of ideas. As well as her husband, Les, for giving her space to draw.

The biggest thank you of all goes to the youth who do the hard work that the rest of us take for granted. We love you and are in awe of you.